MayBe i'M iLL

MayBe i'M iLL

The Shadow in the Empty Chair

By André Goodman

PALMETTO
PUBLISHING
Charleston, SC
www.PalmettoPublishing.com

Copyright © 2024 by André Goodman

All rights reserved

No portion of this book may be reproduced, stored in a retrieval system, or transmitted in any form by any means–electronic, mechanical, photocopy, recording, or other–except for brief quotations in printed reviews, without prior permission of the author.

Hardcover ISBN: 979-8-8229-5458-8
Paperback ISBN: 979-8-8229-5459-5
eBook ISBN: 979-8-8229-5460-1

MayBe i'M iLL

Shadow in an Empty Chair

André Goodman

Existentially Neurotic for Negotiating with an Irrational Mind

Chasing Dreams, Conquering Destiny, Creating Legacy

Simplifying Complexities to a Psychoneurotic Psyche

A Mentally Disturbed Illustration of a Peaceful Mind

Dancing with the Darkness, Navigating in the Night

The Dilemma…the Conundrum…and the Paradox

Calming Down the Alter Ego with Lyrical Poetry

Shadow's Symphony to a Sophrosyne Synopsis

A Melody of Composed Mental Manipulations

Screwing with the Title, Screwed in the Mind

Paralleled Pages of Paradoxical Predicaments

The Client, the Therapist, and the Monster

Perplexed Puzzles-2A-Personal Playlist

Assassinating a Good Man's Character

A Royal Road to an Integrated Mind

After-Thoughts of an Altered Ego

Is This a Dream or Is It My Life?

A Next Level of Consciousness

A Collection of Journal Entries

Thoughts on the 🔑 to My Life

The Truth My Father Told Me

God's Gift and Devil's Curse

An Unformatted Short Story

A Dungeon of Dysfunction

The Freedom to Be MyselF

Shadow in an Empty Chair

The Id, Ego, and Superego

A Counselor's Assessment

A Modern Confrontation

Metaphoric Abstractions

~~14years and 19 days~~

Present Perspectives

Existential Neurosis

Beneath the Iceberg

Paralleled Presence

A Mental Matrix

Light Frequency

MayBe i'M iLL

Calm Your Ego

Korey

The purpose of poetry is to remind us how difficult it is to remain one person, for our house is open, there are no keys in the doors, and invisible guests come in and out at will.
Czesław Miłosz

Table of Contentment

A Counselor's Foreword · xi
A Good Man's Self-Report · xiii
An Assassin's Answer · xvi
Introduction · xvii
A Fantasy Inside Reality · xix

Part 1: A Good Man's PreLude to Death

1   A Good Man's Genesis · 4
2   Heavenly Father, · 5
3   A Good Man's Purpose · 6
4   A Good Man's Story for His Son · 8

Part 2: A Good Man's Football Life

5   A Few Years Prior · 13
6   A Good Man's Headlines · 14
7   A Good Man's Mentality · 16
8   What the F*** Happened to My Leg? · · · · · · · · · · · · · · · 17
9   A Good Man's Prayer · 18
10 The Palmetto Bowl · 21
11 The Catch II/The Push-Off · 22
12 A Good Man's Truth · 23
13 Draft Season · 26
14 A Good Man's Disappointing Ending · · · · · · · · · · · · · · 29
15 A Good Man's Injured History · 31
16 Dying 2B Recognized · 35

Part 3: A Good Man's Reckoning with the Darkness

17	A Good Man's Altered Ego	40
18	A Good Man's Spiritual Awakening	42
19	My First Memory	44
20	A New Year, Same Story	45
21	An Eyewitness to Murder	46
22	An Eyewitness to Attempted Murder	48
23	A Lion's Heart	50
24	My Half Big Brother	53
25	"What you gonna do about it?"	55
26	A Triggered Memory	56
27	Korey	57

Part 4: A Good Man's Altering Ego

28	A Good Man's PreLude to Death	65
29	MayBe i'M iLL	69
30	A Good Man's Fatherly Encounter	72

Part 5: A Good Man's Prerequisite

31	A Good Man's Unconvinced Spouse	78
32	A Good Man's Message	79
33	A Lopsided Love Affair with My Wet Dream	80

Part 6: Shadow in an Empty Chair

34	MayBe i'M iLL by Design	86
35	A Good Man's Next Session	88
36	A Good Man's HaLLs-2-HeLL	89

A COUNSELOR'S FOREWORD

A Good Man walks into my office motivated and inspired by his new revelation, an integrated theory he's testing for the first time through his experimental manuscript. He has been my client for forty-five years, so it isn't the first time he's shared his outlandish aspirational goals. A Good Man retired from a ten-year professional football career twelve years ago, after his youngest child was born. He is a forty-five-year-old black male with desires of becoming a licensed professional counselor (LPC), counseling individuals on mental wellness…although he himself is mentally ill. By his own count, he's had countless concussions, precognitions of other worlds.

A Good Man's presenting issue is his desire for self-actualization. After life in the fast lane, upon his retirement, his professional progress has come to a stifling halt. Unable to adjust to the adversity of his mental state, he has created an imaginary, upside-down pyramid of challenges as his latest innovative intervention. He states that atop his multidimensional pyramid of conflict resides God's promise.

A Good Man is tasked with a mysterious journey to topple the darkness of the pyramid and rescue his life's purpose from his demons. They both await his courageous attempt to conquer his destiny through visualization, a creative work of art asserting his ascension to the next level. It's key in creating his legacy. There is only one path that leads to God's promise, but there's a dilemma.

A Good Man is medically diagnosed with major depressive disorder (MDD), generalized anxiety disorder (GAD), post-traumatic stress disorder (PTSD), attention deficit hyperactivity disorder

(ADHD), and obsessive-compulsive disorder (OCD). When his life experience feels lopsided in relation to his destiny, it instigates paralyzing symptoms, including a persistently low mood, a decreased interest in pleasurable activities, feelings of guilt and worthlessness, a lack of energy, and poor concentration. His adventure is a mental matrix of perplexed premonitions.

A Good Man is in internal turmoil, but he maintains a calm demeanor, although he is easily triggered by the anticipation of conflict. He's been hypervigilant since birth due to his childhood trauma. His monologue is convoluted, but as he vents, I'm actively listening for tidbits of truth in his story. He declares he awakens every day with a single goal in mind: to be better. However, he's unable to shake the dark shadow of psychological disturbances hindering his maturation.

A Good Man's new studies have led him to a gigantic discovery. He reports that maintaining a routine and sustaining consistent discipline in a healthy lifestyle that's uniquely catered to his mental health is his formula for personal progression. In essence, his spirit is granted a new level of consciousness, an updated artificial software that provides him accurate alignment with his passion, purpose, and legacy.

A Good Man must prove his theory by properly illustrating how he's been able to calm his neurotic mind by simplifying the complexities of obsessive thoughts, compulsive acts, and his disconnection from reality. The ability to calm his thoughts permits clarity, allowing God to write his lifesaving story. Before he hands me his new manuscript, he explains his artistic method.

A GOOD MAN'S SELF-REPORT

So I've developed a simple theory to improve my overall health, but it's complex. It focuses on my upside-down hierarchy of needs. The symptoms that complement my mental health disorders can be advantageous if I'm able to redirect the energy. The atrociousness of my neurotic thoughts have the same theme. I'm persistently depressed by the misalignment of my life's experience in relation to my life's purpose, causing a decreased interest in life altogether.

My feelings of irrelevance stem from a lack of purpose, which in turn decreases my daily energy. I'm unable to focus on anything disassociated from my mission to uncover God's promise. The development of an advantageous game plan to compete against the mob of monstrous challenges associated with this treacherous expedition has me agitated, disturbing my nightly sleep routine.

It's a battle for my life, so of course I'm constantly worried about my inability to defeat the dark shadow that stalks me along my way. My skill set is flawed. During my previous attempt at personal and professional evolution, the Silent Assassin threw bombs of traumatic memories that I'd buried long ago. The vivid flashbacks produced nightmares, leaving me trapped in a paralyzed sleep. The intrusive images are intensely distressing, symbolic reminders of why I'm unworthy of the life I desire. To avoid the mental disturbance, I shut down all logic and feed off my instincts only, leading to impulsive behaviors.

I'm always on alert for the next threat. The hypervigilance leads to uncontrollable compulsions that are repetitive. The Dark Shadow implanted plants of worry alongside my charted path, so I'm unconsciously anxious at all times. This is my life. I continue to chase my dreams because it's beneficial in providing a healthy distraction, but it's to the detriment of my reality. That's my paradox in a nutshell.

As a trusted friend once stated, I'm a conundrum manifested… a living enigma, a walking contradiction. He's not wrong. I desire to connect with others but prefer to be alone. I can adapt to any environment, but I don't fit in anywhere. My heart is humble, but my aura occupies a mindset that is borderline arrogant. I'm self-aware of my capabilities but lack patience in any process. I possess enough social skills to navigate the world of business and politics, but I have a low tolerance for the bullsh*t most people offer.

I'm compassionate enough to empathize with others, listen to their stories…and offer solid feedback. I rarely follow my own advice. My reasoning is logical, but my emotions are overpowering. I love helping others, but I'm naturally introverted. I refuse to conform to societal standards, but I desire to be understood. I have a curious mind, but I bore easily…so I rarely explore anything with any intellectual depth. I comprehend the complexities of the human mind, but I have trouble translating my own mental thought processes.

All these things are symptoms confirming my dysfunction. Medically declared mentally disabled, I've begun to question my own sanity, although I've felt this way forever. Until I'm able to format my story into a coherent manuscript, the question remains… MayBe i'M iLL, littered with mental deformities? Or MayBe I'm Still, eternally unbothered? So I research the parallels of the spiritual world as it relates to mental health issues.

The data suggest the impact of spirituality on mental health encourages people to have better relationships with themselves, others, and the unknown. Spirituality can help deal with stress by giving you senses of peace, purpose, and forgiveness. It habitually becomes more important in times of emotional stress or illness.

The Angel's Number has taken on new meaning, since it's all I see lately. It's been speculated that #1111 is a powerful indicator that you are in alignment with the divine guidance and support of your angels. It signifies that you are on the right path and that the universe is conspiring in your favor. This number serves as a reminder to trust your intuition and have faith in the journey ahead. MayBe i'M iLL for believing the nonsense, but I've convinced myself of its truth because it's the only thing that keeps my mind calm. The #1111 is paralleled with the comfort of spiritual encouragement, and I see its natural beauty. My favorite Bible verse states…

> The LORD will fight for you; you need only to be still (Exod. 14:14).

My presenting issue is the danger of self-actualization. When my life experience is misaligned from spiritual guidance, I sit still, hoping God keeps his promise. My most sincere desires are to maximize my potential and to live my life with purpose. I've chosen to maintain faith in God's word, so I must take the next step in this journey, no matter how petrifying. At the bottom of the mountaintop is proof of my sanity. Without it, my survival is questionable. Sleeping next to my destiny is the Dark Shadow Master, my evil twin…the Silent Assassin. The confrontation ignites an identity crisis, and I'm clueless as to which character I'm currently portraying.

This manuscript is a short story about A Good Man's mental health journey of wellness, with a message reminding him to stay true to himself. Its intent is to be his lifesaver! Here, counselor, tell me what you think?

AN ASSASSIN'S ANSWER

I'm not your counselor; you're having another episode. You're still trying to reach an imaginary mountaintop? Supposedly, it's also an upside-down pyramid of confrontations presented as a challenge to your mental health? The silencer on your headphones isn't working, so I can hear your thoughts clearly. It's the same playlist you continue to play nonstop, and it's getting louder. Your Greatest Hits has a theme of hopelessness, and it's intolerable. You're going to have another mental meltdown.

If your Masterpiece is vivacious, the verses will not bail you out. Your fate is already sealed, and you won't last much longer. I suggest you say your last goodbyes. What's happened to you, homie? Your life has fallen apart. You're walking with a permanent limp. You've lost the graceful glide guiding you through this jungle. Did you lose your moral compass as well? Your path is paved already, so why are you hibernating in isolation? Whom are you hiding from? Frankly, I didn't expect to see you again anyway. You were so terrified the last time I saw you, exiting the arena so abruptly after the last contest.

Do you remember how disastrously disappointing you were that day? The battle for our life, and you froze; you choked. You've gotten everything you asked for. You can pretend lifestyle doesn't matter to you, but you can't lie to me; I know better. You enjoy the attention, and you've bought into your own hype, with your hypocritical belief that you are "A Good Man." You look dejected; you look finished, still afraid of astronomical heights. Do you see the multitude of monstrosities in these mountains? You don't possess the skill set to defeat any of them. You're coming into my

HoMe, believing you can challenge Me. You Must be iLL? Let's replay that playlist once again so I can remind you what happened last time. Take a seat.

January 6, 2024ish…

Greetings,
Please take five minutes to proofread the attachment. Spoiler: it's a prelude for what's to come. The story begins with a warning. It'll be tough untangling the word salad, but it's done intentionally. The twisted text is meant to illustrate the twisted thoughts of my mental illness. The objective of the story in its entirety is to transform the experience of trauma and mental health into overall health and wellness, a Better Quality of Life.

 Close to a decade ago, I wrote a poem and posted it on Facebook. I don't usually engage on social media, but I was proud of the art I'd created, and I was finally comfortable talking about Mental Health. I entitled it "MayBe i'M iLL." To date, it's the best literature I've produced, but I shredded it the moment I posted it. I haven't been able to recover it since. I've been irritated for weeks.

 Instead of racking my brain with what I lost, I created Something New. A Collection of Journal Entries. No pressure, but I'm hoping I've outdone myself with this Prelude. It isn't formatted. It's littered with run-on sentences, explicit language, and poor punctuation, but again…it illustrates my cognitive deformities. It's the first entry from my book of poetry; a portrayal of my daily thought processes. I hope you can follow it. I hope you like it.

 I need your honest critique and feedback as educated professionals. Imagine I'm a stranger introducing my work online. Instinctive responses only. Your opinions are my comment section. If you're inspired, feel free to edit. I'm finally extending an invitation into my world. It's the hardest thing I've ever done, and the most excited I've been in a while. Before you proceed, I'll make you a promise. If you can fight through The Intro, it'll be worth it in the end. Here's an Extreme Sample. Please bear with me until The Story Starts.

A FANTASY INSIDE REALITY

"My love affair with words began with lessons learned from lines that painted poetic portraits of my most painful experiences. I empathized with the sounds generating energy to this extremely exhausting existence. The musical reports of my reality are an emotional roller coaster, elevated at foreign heights. It's an endless ride of unrealistic expectations."

These complicated contemplations are managed by A Process that allows for clarification.

Thanks in advance for your consideration,

A Good Man

Part 1:
A Good Man's PreLude to Death

Warning: This short fiction may be difficult to read and tough to decipher. It's unorganized because I'm unorganized. It's an agonizing portrayal of Illogical Illustrations, inadequately formatted, unstructured as well.

The tales consist of Conflicting Characterizations, contradicting one another and communicating in past, present, and future tense. It's a maze of Mystical Absurdities filled with Illiterate Alliterations.

To deliver a comprehensible storyline, I've altered my process. But still, I misinterpret its meaning. Apologies in advance for any confusion thus far; I'm dealing with a few psychological disorders. My cognitions reside in a chaotic universe of distortions.

Wandering aimlessly through the wilderness of an abyss, I encounter A Void of Nothingness. It's the impasse I've impatiently wrestled to avoid. The anticipation of warfare devours the last crumbs of my motivation; I have nothing left to offer as tribute. The penalty: Another Dance with the Darkness. The confrontation will be one-sided.

I've been here before. Ages ago, I negotiated an agreement to pursue my God-given purpose, plus the peak of my abilities. But presently, I'm huddled in hibernation, sentenced to a decade of paralyzed sleep. The dance has commenced.

Episodes of Sleep Paralysis are repetitive cycles of feeling buried while alive, motionless, and unable to speak. However, I'm fully aware of my surroundings, and I'm foolishly anticipating an awakening that never arrives. Stuck in rumination, I'm replaying records and recollections of my life's lowliest moments. The playlist is entitled "My Greatest Hits."

The lyrical tune is painful to my soul, with contents encompassed with failure after failure followed by infinite faults, forcing an examination into fatality. There is no blueprint depicting strategies assisting my ascension to what's above. The Darkness ensues. Scaling to higher heights requires me to become a man I've never known before. Instead of asserting my will, I sit still.

The contemplation of my idled spirit ignites a fire full of fortitude. The blaze illuminates the way, but it's highlighting The Halls to HeLL. Reverberations produce movies of my most traumatic memories. Despite the daunting appearance, the assignment is clearly conveyed. I must journey beyond my discomforts to discover my life's purpose. I'm ordered to chase my dreams, conquer my destiny, and create a legacy…while balancing episodes of neurosis. I'm praying for a miracle. Lord, are you There?

—A Good Man

"A Void of Nothingness"

A GOOD MAN'S GENESIS

Alone in a crowded house late one night, I'm having premature thoughts of death. I envision killing someone when faced with a lack of options. I have visions of dying during a violent struggle. I consider why some consider suicide as an option. Immediately, I ponder the idea of never seeing my mother and sisters ever again. Brokenhearted, I break out into a ball of tears. The thoughts are too much to handle. Is heaven real? If so, do I qualify? I've never attended church, so the concept of God as an all-powerful being baffles me. I'm only thirteen years old. I can't make sense of it all, so I drop to my knees and pray for a miracle. The interaction is revealing. In exchange for God's continual support, I promise to do better and be better by giving all that I am to serve a higher purpose. It's both satisfying and terrifying. The stakes are too high, and I'm uncertain of my ability to live up a flawless standard. Nothing about my thirteen years suggests I'm qualified to be victorious, but often I hear the least of us is often used. The agreement alters my ambitions. As I fall asleep, I experience my first episode of Sleep Paralysis. Lord, are you there?

HEAVENLY FATHER,

I come to you on bended knee, with a humble heart…asking forgiveness for my sins, ones I knowingly and unknowingly commit…

Thanking you for your grace and mercy; your guidance, strength, wisdom…

Thanking you for your presence, thank you for your blessings…thank you for your Son, your word, and your spirit.

Heavenly Father, I pray for health and wellness for myself, my immediate family, as well as extended family and friends.

Father, I ask you for financial abundance. Not to exalt, but to provide, protect, and influence the world around me.

I desire to make you proud. I'm lost without you.

I submit to your will. I surrender to your service.

Guide me to the path that leads to your purpose for my life.

I love you, and I'm grateful for your Love.

In your son's name, I pray for PEACE for all.

AMEN! 🙏

—A Good Man

A GOOD MAN'S PURPOSE

After competing in the National Football League for ten seasons, I retire with the hope of chasing a deferred dream. I've always desired to share my life experience with those with the potential to benefit from it. However, I do not possess a road map, nor am I blessed with a mentor or role model who's paved the path beforehand.

Luckily, a colleague from college offers me a position ideal for the initial part of my plan. I become the director of player development at the University of South Carolina, a position focusing on assisting student-athletes with their transition into college sports and providing personalized support throughout their college careers. This affords me the opportunity to have one-on-one discussions with players regarding both their personal concerns and career prospects.

I hold the position for five years. Afterward, I spend eighteen months working at the local United Way. My mission as the youth program manager: coordinating a community coalition committed to recognizing and responding to the impact of childhood trauma. I'm also given the assignment of planning and facilitating community awareness events on adverse childhood experiences (ACES) to further educate the community on toxic stress.

I'm unfit to be in this position. I'm not educated enough on the subject, but I need to be. During one of the community events that I organize, an agitated eight-year-old boy threatens to kill me. I ask him to leave some cookies for the rest of the group, and he is triggered. I need to learn the details of his situation. I have an inkling his story mirrors my own.

I research resources to better serve an already underserved community, a community in which I'm rooted. To advance my education, I apply to a private academic institution in which I'm able to formulate an idea of future ambitions. I need to become a counselor; there aren't enough black males in the industry. I want to counsel and target an audience of young men, maybe with athletic aspirations providing the perfect icebreaker. I have a duty to help guide these young men who look like me—the kids who are me.

I consult with an older friend who's gone above and beyond to expand my worldview, especially when I was an undergrad. I ask if the considerations are worth my time. His answer is short; he states…it's your obligation. I return to my alma mater, interning as a counselor in training. I'm looking forward to the work.

I'm certain this Statement of Purpose isn't properly formatted, but if this is my purpose, the format in which it arrives doesn't matter. I desire admittance to your program. I'm confident my skills and commitment to professional development make me an excellent candidate.

Thanks for any/all consideration,

—A Good Man

A GOOD MAN'S STORY FOR HIS SON

With my eyes closed and my knees bent, I pray with a heavy heart; my desire to impact the world has gotten off to a rocky start.

Aspiring to convert my thoughts into inspiring wordplay, but struggling to find the importance in what I'd like to say?

Please tell me what tone is proper, in which manner should I speak. Standing with an improper posture while awaiting all critique.

What height should I hold my head; what stance makes the most sense? Careful with all my calculations; I'm hoping you take no offense.

Plenty of divisive issues; there's passion in the politics, but no beauty in the picture painted… please ignore the aesthetics.

What is it about my demeanor that disturbs your sanity? My actions are meant to serve a purpose; there is no value in the vanity.

Whether I stand to salute our colors, or I kneel in defeat…I receive no adequate explanation for innocent bodies in the street.

If I allow you to determine my value, I'll never receive my fair share; fully aware of how the world operates, I don't expect you to care?

Nevertheless, the fight continues; there's still a swagger to my walk. Past generations bear witness; justice cannot be an afterthought.

Hoping for a healthy discussion when all is said and done. I welcome all feedback; I'd like to know What Story to Tell my son?

Part 2:
A Good Man's Football Life

The Story Starts twenty years from the beginning, on September 12, 1998. We are playing the Georgia Bulldogs on national television (ESPN). It's a big deal. Just three years prior, I hadn't even participated in competitive football. Basketball was my love and my greatest inspiration. But now here I am, in complete shock. Before I can properly process anything, I'm thinking my right leg has been amputated. I can't feel pain, but the unfamiliar sensation suggests a demoralizing result. The medical staff is surrounding me, and the stadium grows quiet. I wake up in a hospital, my leg having already been operated on. I must have blacked out.

"What the F*** happened to my leg. Where the F*** is my mother? Where the F*** are my memories? Are my sisters here? What the F*** happened between the stadium getting quiet and me lying here in a post-op room? Did I even have conversations with the doctors beforehand? Where the F*** is my family?"

The procedure is performed the morning following the incident. Torn are my ACL, PCL, and MCL—along with my quad and hamstring muscle and…other insignificant ligaments that feel very significant right now. I'm told the head coach stopped by at some point, but in the commotion, I've already lost track of days, events, and people visiting. Getting around campus isn't an option. I'm unfit to attend classes, so my classes are dropped just as the semester starts. The trip back home to Greenville is deflating. Just a few years prior, I was unfit to be in this position.

A FEW YEARS PRIOR

I've have an appetite for greatness, an intense passion to be something foreign from everything I've known thus far. In the spring before my junior year of high school, my closest buddies, who happen to be twins…convince me to try out for the football squad. Basketball is the only sport I know. Playing football is laughable. In fact, my mom actually laughs when I tell her I'm participating. I mean I get it, I don't even like basic human contact, but the twins' pitch is encouraging. It goes…

> "We know you're quiet by nature, and you prefer basketball over the physicality of football, but if you want to be successful in anything you do, you must take all the anger your soul has suppressed and unleash it every time you step on any battlefield. It's your only way."

It's inaccurately translated, but in my mind, it's what I hear. "It's your only way," repeating constantly. In order to achieve greatness, I must be willing to turn myself upside down and inside out and allow the fear of worthlessness to push me pass my discomforts, toward my best self. I accept the challenge and allow the headlines to tell my story.

A GOOD MAN'S HEADLINES

A Good Man had never played organized football and had little desire to start. He wasn't interested. Basketball was his love. His junior year of high school, friends from the football team talked him into giving it a try, but he wasn't sure he'd stick around.

Two seasons later, his athletic abilities land him a spot in the North-South All-Star game. Football still hasn't risen to the top of his favorite sports, but with his speed, A Good Man has become a quick study. He's planning to sign with the University of South Carolina next month.

A Good Man has the tools but needs the experience. He possess natural skills, but he has a lot to learn. Whether he continues to play receiver or becomes a defensive back, he'll need work to become more physical. A Good Man received a three-week crash course in how to play cornerback in the South-Eastern Conference (SEC). He didn't play much defense at the high school level, so everything is brand-new. But A Good Man is shining. The redshirt freshman from Greenville catches Coach Scott's eye in Friday's practice, picking off two passes. A Good Man is the most athletic guy of the entire freshman class, and he's also been the most impressive, getting better as he transitions to the defensive side of the ball. He has the tools, but he needs spring practice to learn how to play in the secondary. He's already shown speed and toughness.

A Good Man is really beginning to make a move at the cornerback position and seemingly developing some excellent cover skills. The redshirt freshman is also getting good at knocking away praise aimed his way by his coaches and teammates. He doesn't feel he's earned it. He has yet to play a game, and he's competed in the sport for only three years. But he is fast. His 4.31 forty-yard dash ties him for the fastest player on the team, and he's having a great preseason. Hardly a day goes by that Coach Scott doesn't praise his play.

A GOOD MAN'S MENTALITY

I don't recognize who I've become, quietly attempting to murder every challenge that disrupts my aspirations. Despite the lack of experience, despite the redshirt…I'm ready. Now it's time to display the determination to transform my potential into productivity. Regardless of my lack of physicality, if I cover well enough, it won't matter. Cover corners are just as valuable. I get it; tackling is all about desire and technique, but I'll forever remain calculated in my approach. I'll stay after practice each day, studying how I can cater my skill set to fit the team's defensive scheme. Tomorrow I will be better. I must be better. There are no shortcuts to being the best. I don't need the praise or headlines. The respect from my coaches and teammates is enough for me. I just want to crack this starting lineup. The Bulldogs are coming to town in a few weeks. It's a nationally televised game and an opportunity to test my ability against tough competition. With only six months of football experience…I'm ready!

WHAT THE F*** HAPPENED TO MY LEG?

Saturday night the Gamecocks' defensive unit took a devasting blow. Freshman cornerback A Good Man tore multiple ligaments in his right knee in a gruesome collision with Georgia tight end Wiggins. A Good Man underwent surgery Sunday morning. He's certainly lost for the season. The South Carolina cornerback must also undergo a second surgery in the reconstruction of his right knee. With this injury, there is no way of knowing if A Good Man will play football again. With his spare time, he's writing poetry, using words as his release. His poems detail the road he's taken, one that is assuredly less traveled. His verses are also his way of talking with God. He only shares his poems with a select few and has never sought to have any published. It defeats the purpose for his art; he doesn't care for recognition. One poem, entitled "My Prayer," holds a special place for him. He wrote it after his horrendous knee injury, suffered against Georgia in the second game of the 1998 season. Doctors wondered if A Good Man would play football again. As he pondered his future, A Good Man turned to "A Blank Piece of Paper" to jot down his thoughts…

A GOOD MAN'S PRAYER

I close my eyes and exhale; guidance is what I'm looking for…

Thinking the pain couldn't get worse, I guess you felt I needed more…

They said life wouldn't be easy, or at least that's what I was sold…

But even as the sun shines brightest, the world in which I reside remains cold…

And why should I even listen to the things they tell me…

They've never walked my streets; they'll never see what I see…

I became bitter, but bitter I am no longer…

What doesn't kill me can only make me stronger…

I press on for reasons explained easily…

For the father who left, stunned to see who I turned out to be…

I press on for my mother because she's pressed on for me; this I know…

For my sisters, my family; they helped this young man grow…

I feel like I'm ready to meet you; don't get me wrong, this life I love…

But it must be better there with you in the skies above…

All odds against me; this battle I continue to fight…

You blessed me with the heart of a lion; it leads me to the path that's right…

Funny feelings of the world resting on my shoulders; I know that it's not…

It's crazy down here; every other minute, another gunshot…

What am I to do but get on my knees and ask forgiveness for the things I've done wrong…

Strengthen me like you have my mother; she's been through a lot, yet she remains strong…

You've been there beside me, given me more than deserve; I'm grateful for all you've done…

I've been too busy counting my problems and not my blessings; the ride thus far has been fun…

Yeah, it's been hard at times when some of my people you took away…

Feeling lost and abandoned, I heard your voice confirming—it'll be okay…

Scared of failure is something I used to be…

You showed me failure doesn't exist if I'm giving my all to succeed…

Stupid things I did, mad at the world—thinking of things I'd been through…

My mother tells me I'm still alive; many others have it worse than you…

Now I see the world for what it is; I accept and deal with it…

Can't hide from it, hate, greed, envy—I'm learning to live with it…

Please hold me in your arms, Heavenly Father; never let go…

Apologies for pushing you away, but the devil had a tight grip, trying to take my soul…

You came back to get me; that I greatly appreciate…

I'll follow your path to the end, doing right by myself and others, no matter what it takes…

Bitter I was before; bitter I am no longer…

Thou that does not kill me will only make me stronger…

Amen,

—A Good Man

THE PALMETTO BOWL

The Carolina-Clemson state rivalry is a *big* deal. The teams don't like each other, just for the sake of not liking each other. I'm 798 days removed from September 12, 1998. It's the first full season of my college football experience. I'm merely a redshirt junior in title, having played only ten games at the cornerback position. I should be ecstatic to have recovered from such a gruesome injury, but instead I'm stoic. The ability that previously set me apart from my competition is now average at best. Only I know to what extent, but it's enough to dampen my demeanor. I played my worst game last Saturday against the Florida Gators, giving up two touchdowns and a whole lot of yards to Gaffney and Caldwell. I've never felt so deflated until today.

Today we face the Clemson Tigers in my hometown. It's more than a *big* deal. Our seniors have never beaten our in-state rivals, but this year we have a solid team. Had we been victorious the previous week, we quite possibly could have represented the Eastern Division in the SEC Championship game. But in the state of South Carolina, beating your state rival is as sweet as it gets! For fifty-nine minutes and fifty seconds, I'm content with my play after such a poor performance the week prior.

THE CATCH II/THE PUSH-OFF

For the first time since 1987, both teams are ranked entering the game. Trailing late in the game 14–13, Clemson quarterback Dantzler connects with wide receiver Gardner for a fifty-yard reception to Carolina's eight-yard line with ten seconds remaining. Carolina players and fans point to a replay seemingly showing Gardner pushing off Gamecock defender A Good Man, while Clemson players and fans contend that the contact is mutual and incidental. No penalty flag is thrown on the play, leaving the Clemson kicker to kick a twenty-five-yard field goal that gives Clemson a 16–14 win. The game remains divisive, with Clemson fans remembering it as "The Catch II" and Carolina fans remembering it as "The Push-Off Game."

A GOOD MAN'S TRUTH

It felt like a push, enough to impede my play on the football. The reality is that Gardner made a great play, and I should have been better. The two-hour bus ride back to Columbia was the longest two days of my life. Repetitive replays: moment after moment on the nightly news, and again early Sunday morning, Sunday afternoon, Sunday evening, for weeks on end leading up to the bowl game…rapid replays repeating, over and over and over again, until my mind collapsed within itself. In the locker room after the game, I walk up to the seniors to apologize for having not been good enough. Most are teary-eyed. The guilt is unbearable. The media presence afterward is more massive than usual, and I still have to face my family. The details of the next few moments are hazy. The details of the play itself, not so much.

I saw the play coming. Any solid corner knows when he's on a deserted island. Most times I'm comfortable, even when one of the nation's best wide receivers is my only threat. Dantzler rolls to his left, my right, but I'm not fooled. Starring at the other cornerback position is an All-American, my bookend best friend. They are not throwing his way. By my count, I have already defended three deep passes. I'm guessing they watched last week's film of the Gator game.

Woody rolls in the opposite direction; it is the third easy alert, the second being the formation. The first alert, the nearest sideline. I lock eyes with our former head coach, and he's holding a call sheet. I was told he visited me in the hospital 797 days earlier. It all plays out in slow motion. I break away from the final huddle with confidence, as I do most of the time. No matter which sideline is nearest, I'm sure to exude cockiness. No fear. It isn't fabricated. Despite my disability, I still bet on myself every time. Every now and then/again, self-doubt intervenes, but it's usually short-lived. Invincibility is an innate characteristic of a self-declared warrior. Right away, I recognize Gardner aligned as the solo receiver. No problem. I look to Clemson's sideline, accustomed to looking a champion opponent eye to eye.

It's Coach Scott's eyes that I see, surprised to see me competing after experiencing such a horrendous injury. One that he witnessed. Yeah, I know with absolute certainty the play is coming my way, and why I've had to defend so many deep passes all game.

Despite the odds of being the athlete that miraculously transformed himself into a football player, of all things, I can still hear my mother's giggle…I'm ready. I'm ready for whatever, whichever, however, whenever…except for the outcome of that play. It crushed my soul, and I'm uncertain of the revival rate. My first twenty-one years have tested my resilience. I can tolerate the pain usually; my threshold is relatively high until it encompasses the pain of others. The repetitive replays of this life I've lived are rapidly ruining my resolve.

My second full season of competitive football has a rough ending as well. Having experienced a grueling two-year rehabilitation of my right knee, I play the game very cautious and calculating. There is no disguising it; the film doesn't lie. My position coach has taken notice, encouraging me to take part in the friendly 🔥 and to stop standing around the pile. In football terms, he means man up and tackle somebody. I get it. I'm sure Coach Holtz and the entire defensive coaching staff assumes I'm saving myself for a future National Football League career.

We beat the Georgia Bulldogs for the second time in two years in the second game of the 2001 season. The following week of practice, a few assistant coaches allude to NFL scouts considering me as one of the top prospects in the country at the cornerback position! Coach Holtz is legendary regarding his association with college football. He comes to me and tells me I should practice as if I were already a professional player, to raise my standard and elevate my level of play. Coming from Coach Holtz, it is the ultimate compliment and a motivating factor in "My Drive to Be Great."

I thought I'd lost my leg on September 12, 1998. I've played fewer than fifteen games of Division I college football at the cornerback position. With that, I'm considered to be an NFL prospect. None of it feels real, yet I spend 0 percent of my mental energy thinking about professional football. I'm not sure football at any level is in my future. I hate the thought of dragging my leg around the football field, trying to keep up with superior athletes.

When staring at the friendly 🔥, I choose not to participate because I'm not overly committed to sacrificing more of my body to this game. I'm not convinced professional football is a part of my future. I've yet learn to love it. Doing my job as part of a team is what drives me. But telling me to man up is the ultimate insult. I'll show him my heart. The following game, I dislocate my left shoulder in the friendly 🔥 for the first time, just five games short of season's end. I miss the following contest but finish the remainder of the final three games in a shoulder harness.

DRAFT SEASON

We're facing Ohio State for the second consecutive season in a New Year's Day bowl. The Outback Bowl isn't the invitation the Buckeyes play for, but for the USC Gamecocks, we had to produce one of the greatest turnarounds in college football history and hoped to get the invitation. Over the course of the 1998 and 1999 seasons, our team record was one win and twenty-one losses, with the twenty-one losses happening consecutively. So along with the rigorous rehabilitation of my right knee, I watched my team struggle through that experience. Back-to-back victories against a national powerhouse will be a great culmination. I'm unable to get through the first half of the game before dislocating my left shoulder for the second time in what would be my final play of my college football career. Major surgeries were required to both start and end my college football experience.

Devastating, to say the least. Participating in the Senior Bowl game for the NFL scouts isn't an option. Performing at the National Football League combine isn't possible. I can't perform when the NFL team's personnel comes to the university for the Pro Day. I miss it all. Initially, it's no biggie. If I never play another snap of football, it will not be the worst thing. I'm lucky to have recovered from the severity of the right knee injury. The SEC coaches voted me Second Team All-Conference.

Imagine that: four years ago, I didn't know what Southeastern Conference meant to college football; now I'm rewarded with such a prestigious honor. It's enough for me. I'm so deflated from the shoulder surgery so late into the draft process that I'm not sure I have what it takes to pick myself up off the canvas again. But I am who I am. I haven't had the pleasure of rational thinking one day of my life. My heart guides me. It's connected with my natural instincts and attached to my spirit. I trust it; it doesn't lie, even when I lie to myself. Giving in isn't an option. I spend the next four months rehabbing my shoulder, and I return to Indianapolis, the site of the NFL combine, for a second physical examination. They need to test both my knee and shoulder to ensure my sustainability. The physicians analyze every aspect of the two extremities. The grueling exercises and training is a semi-simulation of the two years spent rehabbing from the injuries. I can feel my limitations, so I know they can feel them as well. Fortunately, the right knee is stable, and the left shoulder is healing properly four months after surgery.

I'm able to run the forty-yard-dash ten days or so before the 2002 NFL draft, with seventeen teams returning to campus to work me out as much as I'm able. I'm completely out of shape, having not being able to train, so I barely make it through the workout. I'm able to run an unofficial 4.36 forty-yard-dash. Thanks to my teammates, who were there to not only support me but also to participate in drills for a second time.

I have no inkling of what my NFL draft stock is. My roommate and I watch the draft at Abraham's crib, just he and me, no crowd, no party, no real anticipation. The Carolina Panthers are the first team to call that evening. They're planning to take me with their third-round pick at #73. Of course, I'm ecstatic, playing for the hometown team ninety minutes away from Greenville, South Carolina, easily accessible to the entire family.

I'm fortunate to be considered at all, but the privilege of competing so close to home is a dream come true until call-waiting from an unfamiliar number interrupts. It's draft night, I need to answer it, but what's the proper etiquette in telling the Carolina Panthers to hold on while I take another call, when they're committed to investing in me? The Detroit Lions select me at #68, third pick in the third round. My roommate is drafted with the seventieth pick by the Minnesota Vikings! Now we can party!

A GOOD MAN'S DISAPPOINTING ENDING

I've given up three touchdowns in the only divisional round playoff game I've competed in. It's freezing cold in New England; we're facing Brady's dynasty, and the gravity of intensity is astounding. The assignment I'm given this game is one I've relished since Coach Saban first gifted it to me in 2006. Man-to-man, without help. The first touchdown, our free safety misaligns. I correct the mishap by covering Gronk, although at the snap of the ball, I'm out of position. The result is a magnificent highlight play by two Hall of Fame players. The second touchdown is a sixty-one-yard bomb to former Super Bowl MVP Branch, on a go-route. I'm in press position, and for whatever reason, my fingers are cramping in the cold, causing tightness in my forearm. I'm unable to disrupt him at the line of scrimmage, but I'm not overly panicked. I'm expecting to recover my position, and as I look back to make a play on the ball, I hear it whistle past my ear. A subtle shove prevents me from making the tackle. The third touchdown goes to Hernandez, beating me with a glance route from a tight formation. He has great wiggle for a tight end, and he makes a great play! I think back to all the pregame speeches I've heard over the years. I'm usually immune to the uncontrollable hype, but what I deduce most is…win your one-on-one battle.

Today, I'm on the losing end, and I know it's my last game. I've struggled for the entire 2011 regular season, for unexplainable reasons. No excuses. I did not have the same fluidity in movement. A few years back, I spoke with a teammate about life after losing a step in your natural talents. My misinterpretation of the discussion is quite contradicting, but now I understand. It hits you unexpectedly, but you recognize it from a mile away. There is no denying the diminishing of my athletic abilities. Mentally, I'm not strong enough to endure another setback. Physically, I'm depleted. I've drugged my knee around for twelve seasons of highly competitive football. I have dislocated the same parts of my left shoulder six different times, and I've had five separate surgeries repairing the same capsule in that same shoulder. In my second season with the Miami Dolphins (2007), I'm competing with a loose screw in my left shoulder, hindering 35 percent of the movement and flexibility of my left arm.

A GOOD MAN'S INJURED HISTORY

I dislocated my left shoulder for a second time in the final game of my senior season; it's right before Senior Bowl and NFL Combine season. I'm fortunate to have been drafted, especially after the severity of the right-knee injury. I miss the entire "Organized Team Activities" (OTAs) my rookie season, not practicing until the start of training camp. So I'm behind in preparation from the start. Without being too dramatic, I've yet to fall in love with the game of football. I'm in love with the man-on-man, one-on-one competition. It's the only part of my individual game that gets me excited, but of course it takes a back seat to my role in the team's game plan. I arrived in Detroit with an impaired right knee and a damaged left shoulder, spending what feels like 75 percent of my reps covering flatland and tackling any/everything showing up in my flat zone. Long story short, everything shows up in the flat zone because that's how the defense is designed. Not only am I suffering from the poor team results, but I'm also missing a lot of tackles, and I dislocate my left shoulder for a third time after a solid rookie year!

Research states…I have been limited to visual reps for more than half of my football career. My final year in Motown, I come to understand that the Miami Dolphins inquired about a trade for me. The Lions didn't accommodate. I'm unsure why, seeing that I've fallen to the bottom of the depth chart? Going into the 2006 off-season, I'm a free agent and a third-tier corner at best. Not overly disappointed, I still think highly of myself. I've missed a lot of games, and visual reps didn't sharpen my instincts quite as well as the physical reps.

I truly begin to understand the game of football during the off-season of my fifth year in the NFL. The Miami Dolphins sign me in free agency. During my visit I'm told why. Coach Saban thinks I have solid feet, ideal for man-to-man concepts. He attempted to trade for me the year prior. I don't know who Coach Saban is or what he's about, but day one, within the first fifteen minutes, I learn everything I need to know. Coach Saban is detailed to his core; he absolutely hates missteps. He's the ultimate perfectionist, and I love it!

The 2006 Miami Dolphins have a contending roster. It's the year Culpepper is selected over Brees. Doesn't feel like a big deal. We open the season on the road against the Steelers, in very sloppy conditions and, of course, with a hostile crowd. It's a nationally televised Thursday-night game. We have their offense in third and long, and I get a hands-to-the-face penalty. Automatic first down, Steelers. Now we're in fourth and short; their offense has big personnel on the field. I automatically look to the sideline because I am not usually in on plays with less than two wide receivers in the game. I line up on the closed side with wing tight ends. The ball is definitely coming my way. Sure enough, everyone else is blocked up, and it's just me and the running back. I hesitate to fill the void in the defense. I'm not sure I even get in on the tackle. First down, Steelers. We lose 28–17.

Coach Saban has a system of team accountability; it's so f***ing awesome. It's a visual chart verifying a player's performance, and it's on display for entire building to see. My first game with the Dolphins is a poor performance, so Coach Saban calls me in and presents me with a challenge. I don't say a word. My misinterpretation of his speech...

> "A Good Man, I'd imagine you'd like to gain the respect of your Hall of Fame teammates because they've set a very high standard. I need you to want to tackle the running back."

My six full seasons of competitive football have been agitating. Having experienced a grueling two-year rehabilitation of my right knee and dislocating my left shoulder three times in two years, I play the game very cautious and calculating. There is no disguising it; the film doesn't lie. Coach Saban has obviously taken notice, encouraging me to take part in the friendly 🔥 and to stop standing around the pile. In football terms, he means…"Stop being a p***y and tackle somebody, or man the f*** *up*"! I get it. I'm sure Coach Saban and the entire defensive coaching staff assumes I'm saving myself for a future National Football League career, and he's right.

When staring at the friendly 🔥, I choose not to participate because I'm not overly committed to sacrificing more of my body to this game, although I'm convinced professional football is a part of my future. I'm beginning to love it. When you call me a p***y without calling me a p***y, I'll show you my heart. In our home game against the Titans, playing Cover 2, I read the tackle block down perfectly. I take off to get inside of the receiver's block. I make the tackle near the LOS, close to the tackle box, where all the danger lurks, and I grade out a winner!🔥

In our contest against the Jets, I dislocate my left shoulder in the friendly 🔥 for the fourth time, just six games into the season and a fifth time on Christmas Day, our second game against the Jets that same season. It officially ends my year. I dislocate my left shoulder for the sixth time during off-season OTAs. Five shoulder surgeries in five years and playing on a right knee that's finally starting to feel better, but Coach Saban leaves in the off-season.

Coach Saban, I've actually had a few opportunities to tell you what it meant for me to play for you, but I didn't want to be a burden. I stayed silent instead. Here's my chance. The fact that you absolutely saw my every misstep, took your intolerance, and corrected me ignited a 🔥 inside me I forgot existed. Absolutely, I want all my teammates to respect my effort, but for me it's usually all give and no take. If I am to do what you're asking, chances are it'll be my last game. I know my shoulder is ready to come out again, because I can feel it with the slightest movement. But if it's what the team requires, the only thing you need to know about me…I'll risk it all for one Moment of Greatness.

That fact, balanced with my calculating thought process, allows me to compete for ten seasons in the National Football League, starting nearly 75 percent of games I participate in. I get to play with Hall of Famers and Pro Bowlers, meeting some of the best people and coaches, finishing my career in the defensive backfield with my closet teammate, along with Dawk and Champ. F***ing awesome! After my poor performance in the playoff game against the Patriots, I'm deciding to hang them up. There is no amount of money that can heal losing another step in my abilities. My youngest son is born; I'd like to at least help raise one of my kids. To the rest of my babies, I owe apologies for not being there enough or sometimes at all.

Recently, I've been hit with a shocking wave of depression, although at the time, I'm unfit to identify the pain. It's somewhat baffling. I'm content with my decision to walk away from football, but mentally I'm broken beyond repair. Suddenly I'm disgusted with everyone and everything, most of all myself. I voluntarily walk away from football, and I involuntarily walk away from the game of life. Choosing to stay on the sideline, avoiding the shame of coming up short in becoming the man I think I'm supposed to be. Now I'm stuck in hibernation and confined to this paralyzed sleep. Lord, are you there?

DYING 2B RECOGNIZED

Former Eastside High School standout A Good Man will represent South Carolina as a member of the 2015 Southeastern Conference Legends Class. A Good Man, a four-year letterman, started two years for South Carolina at cornerback from 1997 to 2001. He finished his career with four interceptions, eighty-six tackles, and twenty pass deflections. He earned second-team All-SEC honors from the league coaches as a senior and was named to the SEC Academic Honor Roll in 1999 as a sophomore.

A Good Man was a third-round pick of the Detroit Lions in the 2002 National Football League Draft. He played ten years in the league with Detroit, Miami, and Denver, collecting 342 tackles, a sack, and nineteen interceptions. He currently serves as the director of football student-athlete development at South Carolina.

> (Fade In)…Eastside's A Good Man an SEC Legend for USC
>
> (Fade In)…South Carolina's A Good Man highlights the South Carolina Athletic Hall of Fame's Class of 2017…
>
> (Fade In)…A former South Carolina defensive back is receiving a standout honor…
>
> (Fade In)…A Good Man named to SC Athletic Hall of Fame…

(Fade In)…On Thursday, it was announced that A Good Man, a former Gamecocks cornerback and South Carolina's current director of football development, will be inducted into the South Carolina Athletic Hall of Fame...

(Fade In)…Greenville County Schools honors illustrious graduates. A Good Man was one of six Greenville County Schools graduates inducted into the district's first Hall of Fame…A Good Man and his wife share a blended family…

    Humbly honored, yet it reads like an obituary, an evening news headliner. My life's legacy inscribed in encrypted code. For so long I've wanted to narrate the neurotic nightmare that terrorizes my memory. I awaken daily astray from actuality, chasing the greatness of a shadow that's equipped with knowledge of an insatiable outcome. Yet and still, I yearn for the unknown. It's an infectious illness, though not contagious. All others are uniquely immune. My mornings are pleasant. The bluebirds are chirping, the breeze is calming, and the waves are alleviating, but my mind is mangled with mystery. I'm agitated by an anonymous algorithm, haunting hallucinations prying for purity. Perpetually pondering peaceful Proverbs from life's greatest literature; however, they no longer pacify my pain. I'm dying internally at an agonizing pace.
    Rain showers accompany the New Year's arrival, an impermanent ambience for an isolated mood. There's a soothing symphony antagonizing the catastrophic disaster residing within, producing a balanced melody. Intense winds instigate the traumatic trembling of moderately constructed windows. The thunder's roar interrupts my emotional rhythm as the lightning ignites mystical perspec-

tives that are eager to arrange twelve notes between an octave of self-celebrated fiction.

I'm conceptually constrained by clumsy calamities. My personal beliefs are compulsively barricaded. There's a majestic spirit working on my behalf, although it has mistakenly equated insufficient incentives as possible progression. I'm beginning to question its methodology. I'm deserted in a cage of nonexistence, reflecting on the yesterday's regrets and tomorrow's worries. My consciousness is currently chaotic from the cloudy overcast. I'm overwhelmed by this unbearable burden, relentless in its will to live life on its own terms. The heavenly vibrations glamorize my genius, opposing all rhetorical rejections, granting short glimmers of sunlight.

Yet and still…I've chosen to ignore the world around me. It's consumed with its own massive list of priorities. My name has been excluded from its inventory, an irritant in its entirety. I'm alone, and it's this single commentary that triggers a desperate campaign for care. There's no shortage of cautionary tales, but none are uniquely catered to my disposition. Extreme anxiety has altered society's assessment of my private plight. Pharmaceuticals have become the single solution to even my odds of survival.

In this unexplored moment, I'm anticipating the arrival of an unidentified essence with inarticulate thoughts, known for its ridiculous rambling. Dyslexic dialect narrates the neurotic nightmare occurring in my mind at its convenience, comingling fantasy, and reality. It provokes psychotic principals, unruly in their character. Recognized for its expedited pace, arriving is a gentleman detailed in duplicated description, a prototypical depiction of myself. The Silent Assassin.

Life can only be understood backwards but must be lived forwards. —Soren Kierkegaard

Part 3:
A Good Man's Reckoning with the Darkness

My greatest fear has materialized; the man in the mirror frightens me most. His reflection is limited to a list of deficiencies. With no love for life, he's lost the ability to camouflage his condition. The persona he created for personal protection is incapable of integration with obscurity, leading to a lengthy period of self-destruction. Involuntarily retired from the optical illusions, he's bewildered and belligerent, and he's begging for mercy. His desires are unknown, his days filled with dread, and he's disgusted by his existence. Lacking the capacity for pleasure; he's losing to the internal warfare, and anhedonia is accelerating. Longing for nothing other than silence, he's isolated in images of emptiness. This isn't going to end well. He struggles to outrace his reality, while his friend frantically races up thirty-five flights of stairs to check his weapon for ammunition. He envisions death by suicide.

A GOOD MAN'S ALTERED EGO

I'm being raised by a single mother and two older sisters. I don't know my father, but I do have seven uncles. My favorite uncle, the one I see most, has become a drug addict. Of the other six, the oldest went to the military and did thirty years in the navy. He's high-ranking. Another is an alcoholic and died at in early age from liver failure. Two have been incarcerated for the majority of my upbringing, and one struggles with mental health issues. The one my mother has told me I'm most like, I never got a chance to meet. As I understand the story, he went missing years ago, but apparently my mother has proof that he isn't dead. Either way, it's too much for an eight-year-old to have knowledge of. My very first memory from infancy, I was in the line of fire. Someone drove by our home and shot at my entire family. I remember hearing the tires screech, coming around the curb. I vividly remember seeing a beer bottle burst off a car. On this day, most of my uncles are present. One of them actually returns fire. My mother is on the porch with her closest friends. No one ever talks about that day, so maybe it's just a reoccurring nightmare that continuously interrupts my sleep. Eventually the nightmare turns into sleep paralysis, which is a very common sleep disorder, but my episodes are causing intense fear and anxiety. Whether awake or asleep, there's sudden incapacitation. My body is in shock and powerless. I'm breathing and thinking, but I'm unable to speak. The paralysis may last for seconds or minutes, but as I get older, I'm experiencing them more frequently. Ultimately, I learn to relax my body, calm my mind, and release the fear. I'm dealing with them still. It's still very disturbing, but the force it takes to calm the storm has subsided. My social anxiety is so bad. The slightest bit of chaos causes emotional earthquakes, inner trembles, and a pounding heart rate. Every other day, I'm mentally debilitated.

A GOOD MAN'S SPIRITUAL AWAKENING

Thursday, January 11
1:11
🔔 6:30 AM

A Truth That Filled the Void, January 11, 2024 (1:11:1:11)…
A Star Is Born

Talent comes everywhere. Everyone is talented, but having something to say and a way to say it so people listen to it, that's a whole other bag. And unless you get out there and you try to do it, you'll never know. That's just the Truth. If there's one reason we're supposed to be here, it's to say something so people wanna hear it. Don't you understand what I'm trying to tell you. If you don't dig deep in your f*cking soul, you won't have legs. If you don't tell the truth out there, you're f***ed. All you got is you and what you wanna say to people, and they are listening right now, and they're not gonna be listening forever; trust me. So you have to grab it, and you don't apologize; you don't worry about why

MayBe i'M iLL

they're listening or how long they're gonna be listening for; you just tell 'em what you wanna say. Cause how you say it is the stuff of angels. Music is essentially twelve notes between any octaves. Twelve notes and the octave repeats. It's the same story, told over and over…forever. All any artist can offer the world is how they see those notes.

—Jackson Maine

1978ish…

MY FIRST MEMORY

I'm glad I didn't die, but the memory of that day summoned a dark shadow that haunts me still. I stepped out of the front door to take in my first breath of fresh air. My mother is sitting on the porch with her closest friends, while my uncles are drinking in the yard. It's seldom that we're all together; my family is enjoying a great day. I can see a dude speed around the corner with disastrous intentions. Acutely alert, I watch frame by frame as the shooter gets closer. Time slows down, and the cannon sounds—*boom, boom, boom.* Multiple shots let loose. A beer bottle bursts on the car near the curb where my uncles are standing. My mother and her friends scatter from Imminent Death; it's here, and I'm defenseless. The heat-seeking bullets are mimicking my every move. Haunted by the hallucinations, a beautiful first memory, now the never-ending nightmare of my life, and I'm confined to a paralyzed sleep, "A Prisoner to My Own Story."

January 1, 2024…

A NEW YEAR, SAME STORY

I can hear my youngest son screaming with his friends over a video game. He and his entourage have finally conquered the final quest in their latest adventure. He's in his comfort zone. Elated by the results, he's oblivious to history, my history. He's never known my tumultuous past. It's one of my proudest achievements. Simultaneously, I'm listening to a close family friend explain to my eldest son how he recently murdered a man. He describes "His Struggle." He talks about potentially losing his life in the initial moments of the battle. He is restricted by the front seat of his vehicle. He's in shock, shocked by the assailant's decision to deprive him of the nothingness he possesses. He concludes his story, the sensation he felt when pulling the trigger and the tremors that pierced his spirit. His depiction filled with pain and fear. Understandably so, he almost lost his life. The finale capped off with heartache and terror. Justifiably so, another young man lost his life. Another life taken.

Makes me think about the first time I witnessed murder.

1985ish…

AN EYEWITNESS TO MURDER

I watched a dude get shot in the face today, in the place I call home. It's my block, it's my hood, it's my project. It's the summer break, it's early, and Mom is working as usual. She makes a living at the nearby animal shelter. It's within walking distance. I've made the trip a few times on my own. Sometimes I'd ask for her when I arrived. Other times, I'd just turn around. I'm too frightened to be a burden. In the presence of my mother, I'm good, I'm safe, and I'm special!

My two big sisters watch over me while Mom is gone. I know they love me in their own tough way, taking my best interests into account most times. Although I'm still unsure why they insist I stay outside all day, alone. It's the City Heights Projects? Oh yeah, I remember. They don't like the way I smell when I come inside; I smell like outside.

My love for basketball may get me killed. The nearest b-ball court is a few blocks over. My one general rule when Navigating the Projects is "do not pass through blocks in which you don't reside unless you're with a friend of that specific block." The problem is, I don't have any friends, none that love b-ball the way I do. F*** it, I'm going anyway.

I reach the halfway point just in time to witness the driver reach for their weapon before reaching their arm out of the car-door window, firing a single shot, *boom.* I watch the body drop. Another life taken.

Despite appearances, I am protected by my family. I don't know my father, but I wish I did. I wish I knew what kind of man he was. I wish he were around so often that I'd miss him when he went MIA. It isn't meant to be, so the Go-To Move…"It's best not to think about it; it's best not to care."

Where are my grandparents? Do I have grandparents? I see no images anywhere. I think my mother's parents are dead, and I'm unsure about The Other Side. I wish I could bridge that gap, although I wouldn't know what to expect, so the Go-To Move… "It's best not to think about it; it's best not to care."

I have the best uncles in the world! My Uncle Alexander is my favorite. He's the baby of the bunch. He's the one I see most, and he's by far the coolest person I know. There are always beautiful women in his presence. He's an addict now. I'm unsure how many uncles I have; a few of them are behind bars. They'll be incarcerated for a while.

My Role Models are either locked up, strung out, or nowhere to be found. I guess I'm not a priority. The current head of my household is currently attempting to murder my mother in front of me.

1990ish…

AN EYEWITNESS TO ATTEMPTED MURDER

I don't care for my mom's boyfriend; he rubs me the wrong way. He grabbed me aggressively once when I was younger, leaving my arm swollen and feeling broken. He and I will never share a positive moment. I should tell Mom that he's snorting cocaine when I'm coming home from school, but I think she knows already. It's probably the reason she cries as often as she does while shaking uncontrollably. It's tough getting her to calm down, one of the scariest sights to see.

"Mom, please calm down and stop shaking so much. Mom, Mom, please calm down and stop shaking so much. Ma, Ma, it's me, your baby boy. Please calm down and stop shaking so much."

I know dude has something to do with it. The hate in my heart is growing stronger, but in the following days, everything is back to normal. What the f*ck? This isn't normal. Eventually the dude will witness my wrath. His drug problem is getting out of hand. Every Friday, he's fighting my mother for the rent money? It is the *rent* money, bro, the rent we pay to stay in this house. Why are you asking my mother for our *rent* money? He usually gets his way, but tonight my mother said, "No!" Finally, she's had enough. Then, his two hands wrap around her neck, her two feet dangling two feet from the floor. He's strangling my mother. He doesn't seem to mind that I'm watching, meaning I'm the one eyewitness to this act. I'm helpless to defend my mother, and there's a pretty good chance I'm next. If this is my life, I don't want it. It's making a monster out of me.

1991ish…

A LION'S HEART

After the shooter swirled around the curve and sped down our alley with murderous intentions, the memory never escaped me. I was eight years old when I witnessed a gentleman's lifeless body hit the pavement. The neighborhood in which I spent my childhood educated me on executive decision-making, making the horrifying decision to walk to the park to play a game that supported my dreams.

I'm disturbed by my uncles' addictions and incarcerations. I'm disturbed by the absence of my father. I'm disturbed by the father figure attempting to murder my mother in front of me. I'm most disturbed by the violence my heart is absorbing. A monster sleeps in the master bedroom adjacent to my own, creating a monster out of me. Predators are on the corners of the curbs by the basketball courts where I spend most of my time. Still, b-ball is a beautiful outlet; I don't need anyone else to enjoy it. I can spend entire days attempting to mimic MJ's moves. I'm getting good at it too. When the boys from the block are present for public entertainment, they tease me about my skills…

> "You should be good; you spend the majority of your time on this court, alone—in the rain, the heat, the cold. That's why you're not missing shots."

It isn't meant to be a compliment. They are basically telling me to get a life. Not once will I reply to the insults, because I know what these guys are about. My best friend was present on the day of the infamous drive-by shooting. Now he's a corner-boy, constantly confronting any would-be adversary who has the courage for conflict. He committed his first murder before I left for college. This is my competition. So yeah, I remain a recluse for the most part, secluded in solitude until my passion to play ball takes over. My rebuttal to the subtle slights remains internal, arrogantly whispering aloud to myself blunt statements like…"If getting a life means having your life, give me my life, all day, every day."

I grew up in Greenville, South Carolina, for the first eighteen years of my life. For the first eighteen years of my life, I avoided my city to the point that my sisters' friend group didn't know they had a little brother. I'm afraid for my life every day of my life. The fear isn't strictly petrified feelings of being victimized. I'm also afraid of what I'd do if I'm ever cornered or feel endangered and unprotected. I have been terrified of life since I watched the beer bottle burst on the car near the curb where my uncles were standing, having thoughts of my immediate family losing their lives in that moment. Witnessing a man lying dead on your block is enough to scare any eight-year-old kid. I was twelve years old when I thought my mother was going to lose her life at the hands of the man acting as my father.

I have been afraid for my life every day of my life, but you would never know it. I disguise it well with an impenetrable outer core, and plus, by the age of thirteen, I know I'm a killer. I've become my life experience. It's impossible to dismiss the evil holding hands with my heart. The energy to suppress the destructive parts of my being inadvertently slaughters pieces of my good-natured spirit, making it tough to reconcile with myself. It's casting an invasive Shadow. Now I am the monster that I fear, avoiding conflict and confrontations at all costs, just to preserve my purpose. There are benefits to being this beast. The lionhearted pursuit of passion and purpose makes me feel alive. There is a beauty to being trapped at the bottom of this void. Although I'm shielded from the sun, it only takes a glimmer of hope to rise above the madness. My desire is to be a beacon; a bon🔥 that inflames. I'm hoping the speck of light is enough to strengthen others to do the same.

MY HALF BIG BROTHER

Over thirty years later, the memory finally returns. My half brother is selling heroin at fourteen years old, and he keeps a sawed-off shotgun in our crawl space. Times spent with my half brother are a bag of mixed reactions. We are always patrolling other community projects. He doesn't give a f*ck about his life, and I'm right here beside him. I know who my half brother is; he's the kid that terrorizes me. He's my roommate. Trips to the other neighborhoods are worldly experiences, authentic views of new actualities. The sawed-off shotgun is a necessity.

I'm thirteen years old and already a killer, but only in my fantasy. I want someone to feel my fictitious fury. I'm not afraid of getting cornered. I'm afraid of making my father figure my first victim. But one day the decision will be him or me; I like my odds. If I lose, I'm going out on my own terms.

I hate my half brother; the two or three times I'm in real trouble, it's because I'm impersonating my half brother because I admire my half brother; he doesn't give a f*** about his life. My peers fear him so much that I'm embarrassed by my half brother. He's bullying school kids for their lunch money. I'm in classes with these kids, and I'm getting all the gripes.

> "A Good Man, can you please tell your brother—wait, how is he your brother? Anyway, can you please tell your brother to leave us alone?"

Students are astonished that our bipolar-opposite personalities are related, so I don't call him my brother; his father is not my father. Thoughts about his father make me hate the worst parts of my myself because I'm either (1) terrified, or (2) homicidal. But my half brother always has my back. In third grade, two kids move in on the block. The older brother is cool, but the younger brother, Virgil, is a bully; he's not the one to be messed with. I'm told he keeps a razor under his tongue. I believe the stories because my family's history is littered with identical tales. My greatest fear of a full-fledged fight is getting sliced in the face with a razor blade. I've heard too many familiar stories, and I've seen enough evidence to support what are now nightmares to me! It takes a full year before Virgil finally challenges me. The skirmish is as small as me saying something like…

"If you touch me with that pencil one more time, I'm going to punch you in the face."

I mean it when I say it, without thinking about the consequence. And because Virgil is Virgil, he touches me with the pencil and says…

"WHAT YOU GONNA DO ABOUT IT?"

I'm committed to the punches before he finishes his sentence. I catch him with my best one-two jabs to the face. Virgil pops right up! We're in the middle of a crowded cafeteria. Virgil rushes me and scoops me. It's not the position I want to be in, but before he's able to calculate his next move, my big brother is on top of Virgil. I'll follow my big brother anywhere. I know he'd risk his life for me, but there is no reciprocity. My half big brother might also be the one to kill me someday, especially if I follow through on this plot to murder his father! My big brother is now wanted for attempted murder; I guess we're one and the same! I never knew how to refer to the only brother I know.

A TRIGGERED MEMORY

City Heights Projects apartment 13-B is easy enough to remember when I needed to get back home. There are two brothers living next door with their parents in 13-A. They're cool kids. We've hung out in the front yard a few times, roamed around in our little areas. We're close enough to be considered as friends. I just got news that the older brother has been arrested for killing a cabdriver. I have two immediate questions: (1) murder?, (2) the f***ing cabdriver?

> Strength isn't given; it's grown…when we choose not to surrender to our hardships.
>
> —Commando

1995ish…

KOREY

When I was introduced to Korey for the first time, I knew he was disturbed. He's a few years younger, but he and I grew close, mainly due to the closeness of our residences. He's my neighbor. Our bedroom windows are ten feet apart from each other. Korey is a troubled kid, and I'm troubled by the knowledge of his childhood trauma. His biological father murdered his mother, supposedly when he was too young to remember. Shortly after, his father committed suicide; all the while, Korey was present. Family debates focus on Korey's awareness of the incidents of his infancy.

He is adopted by his uncle, whose wife happens to be best friends with my mom. Korey has behavioral issues; he struggles in school, throws tantrums, and is susceptible to meltdowns, and he's exceedingly defiant. His talents are not evident. He displays no unique skills, and he acquires a learning disability. Korey yearns for attention. He shares notions of his craving often. Korey understands me and my wishes as well. I'm motivated by being more than the mayhem in our avenues. We are bonded by the distance we keep from our peers who are playing loosely with their lives.

I'm unacquainted with my influence; by his accounts, I'm an inspiration to my friend. He follows me to the basketball court one day and voices similar wishes of becoming more than what our block offers. During the summer months, while our parents are working and our siblings are watching over us, I will occasionally slide the bedroom curtains open and check in on my friend. I let him know I notice him; I see him, and he has my attention.

On a few different occasions, I recognize a noose hanging from his closet door, demonstrating the plan he is considering. It scares me to think about the possibilities of what he'll do to himself, so I rush over to make his siblings aware, or do I? Either way, I obviously don't convey the seriousness of the situation. Korey commits suicide at the age of fifteen. He hangs himself in his bedroom closet. I live with the guilt, StiLL. More than once, he'd given proof of his deadly impulses. To his family, sorry for your loss. Please accept my sympathies because apparently, my influence wasn't enough.

Korey, I miss you, buddy, and now I empathize with your pain. 🥺 PS: I discovered your unique skill and talent. You possessed the greatest gift of all: being a great friend!

Tell me a story. In this century, and moment, of mania, tell me a story. Make it a story of great distances, and starlight. The name of the story will be Time, but you must not pronounce its name. Tell me a story of deep delight.

—Robert Penn Warren

Part 4:
A Good Man's Altering Ego

Off to College…and off my block and out of my city for the first time, without a compass. I have no awareness and no rhyme or reason to avoid losing control. The slightest bit of commotion is painful to my psyche, and my organized thoughts during moments of reflection are now chaotic and bunched. I'm utterly dependent on others telling me where to go, what to do, and who to be while publicly performing in front of eighty thousand strange fanatics incessantly evaluating, judging, and assessing me. Every social situation is uncomfortable, and every audience aggravates my anxiety. Plus, my career prospects, at least from my perspective, are based on the improbable probability of becoming a professional athlete in a sport I've yet learn to play. To begin my training, a three-week crash course testing my physical toughness? How can I maintain an eagerness for an unsought afterlife and simultaneously retain an attitude for excelling? I have no rules to live by, and the go-to move is rendered ineffective when defended by my insatiable appetite for self-actualization. It's best not to think about it; it's best not to care. Except, all I do is think about it, and it's impossible not to care.

Instinctively, I adapt by producing a personality fit for protection. He's effectively everything I've never wanted to be. I'm ashamed and unworthy of every blessing ever given to me, pretending to be someone I'm not, which is nothing like me. A Good Man, awkward and confused, modified by a false life. Though full of inferior feelings, they're disguised well by a false mindset of superiority. Please allow me to reintroduce myself, an apparition approved and authorized as an altered ego. A Silent Assassin, appointed to stealthily eradicate every assignment that misaligns with my ambitions.

Postretirement…from the NFL in 2012, I know I want to write something, but I'm unsure how to convey my feelings, mainly because I can't explain what I'm feeling. Although I enjoy writing poetry, I haven't been writing anything for a while now. I begin journaling instead, but my words are interchanging, my sentences are incomplete, and my thoughts are repetitive. I'm confused by the complexity of it all. My mind is racing with entangled thoughts of life's existential meaning. As I write, I'm researching synonyms and their meanings—creating a rabbit hole of discovery. I'm desperately trying to understand this unfulfilling state of mind I'm in. It's hindering both my personal and professional development.

I'm losing aspirations for advancement; I'm losing motivation for everything, and my attitude is no longer self-controlled. I'm trapped inside my mind with no escape. I attend a few NFL Player Development programs: (1) Harvard Business School, and (2) the Wharton School of UPenn. I learn to simplify my complexities. It helps slow the nonstop self-sabotaging, but I'm becoming undone. It's the first day of the week, my first day as player development director for the University of South Carolina Athletics Department. It's not a good day. I'm dropping my eldest son off at school. He needs to be there by 7:45 a.m. With the school being five minutes from the football training facility, I arrive thirty minutes early for the 8:30 a.m. meeting. I have full access to the stadium, but I don't enter the building. I can't enter the building, due to a familiar feeling of panic rushing through my body. I'm frozen in self-reflection, *again!*

How did I get here? Why am I here? What's the point of it all? Similar sensations are often present before performances. As I write this next sentence, I'm realizing why. When I'm in positions of discomfort, it usually means I'm unable to be myself, meaning I once again must perpetrate a character and transform my persona to adapt to a position of comfort. The transformation causes panic attacks. Without a father figure to provide guidance, I've come to grips with the strain of trampling through this 🔥 alone, never learning how to calm myself. It takes a while, converting my character. The first team meeting consist of the coaches, academic advisors, athletic administration, and football personnel. Coach Spurrier is a superior football mind and an even better character for comical commentary. It lightens the mood in serious moments. His gift of gab makes for an interesting experience. I'm unacquainted with the staff, other than the college colleague who recommended me for the position. If I were able to hand-pick my ideal position postretirement, director of player development for my alma mater is atop the list. Yet I'm uninterested in being here. I'm too busy reminiscing on life experiences.

During these critical times, when constrained by internal conflict, a shadow leaks out into the light. Compelled by darkness, it must be confronted. It's another contest against the ultimate warrior. These self-encounters are aspiring competitions designed to decide the direction of my distortions. The contemplations convert into self-dialogue with a shadow, debating who I'm supposed to be at this point. Throughout these confrontations, I'm staring at self-portraits while revisiting past variants to uncover a path not taken. I'm searching for a way out? The path that lights up is highlighted as the Halls to Hell. The inscription on the mirrored walls reads, "Mortal combat vs. traumatizing memories; your death is certain." Take the leap of self-destruction! As I climb I stumble into a free fall where my life flashes before me on a Jumbotron. It's a recycled list of my failures, validating my current state. My thoughts are indistinct, and the isolated safety net is an invisible darkness. With words as my only weapons, I exhibit my faith with witty verses by data-dumping my mental distortions on paper through self-dialogue and label it a "PreLude to Death."

A GOOD MAN'S PRELUDE TO DEATH

Warning: This short fiction may be difficult to read and tough to decipher. It's unorganized because I'm unorganized. It's an agonizing portrayal of illogical illustrations inadequately formatted, unstructured as well. The tales consist of conflicting characterizations contradicting one another, communicating in past, present, and future tense. It's a maze of mystical absurdities filled with illiterate alliterations. To deliver a comprehensible storyline, I've attempted to alter my process, but even still, I misinterpret its meaning. Apologies in advance for any confusion thus far; I'm dealing with a few psychological disorders.

My cognitions reside in a chaotic universe of distortions, wandering aimlessly through the wilderness of an abyss. I encounter a void of nothingness. It's the impasse I've impatiently wrestled to avoid. The anticipation of warfare devours the last crumbs of my motivation. I have nothing left to offer as tribute, and the penalty is death, an eternal sleep. It's the last dance with my demons. A blaze illuminates the way to heLL. Reverberations produce movies of my most traumatic memories. Despite the daunting appearance, the assignment is clearly conveyed. I'm praying for a miracle. Lord, are you There?

I'm losing touch with reality, attempting to survive this nightmare. My method for survival is a fictitious story I sell to myself to get through present moments, but the plot keeps shifting. The involuntary journey is an elaborate web of uncertainty, decorated by my ignorance. I know I'm flawed, but will these faulty feelings condemn me forever?

Is peace of mind possible, despite the disapproval and the invalidation of my worthiness? I'm only thirteen years old; I'm pondering the existential meaning of it all. The weight is too heavy to endure. If it ends today, will I care? Will I be reunited with my mother and sisters in the afterlife? The thought of their absence brings me to tears. My brain can't tolerate many more premature mirages. I need to get some rest.

As I sleep, I can see and hear the world moving all around me, but I can't move, and my eyes are wide shut. Efforts to awake by asserting willpower exacerbate the strain, and the free fall is frightening. I'm dying in this nightmare, which unintentionally has become my horror story. I can't fight back without judgment. The uncivilized anger that anchors me prevents me from giving in to this dilemma. Surrendering isn't in my nature. I've survived worse, although I didn't expect to have to dodge so many bullets at such an early age.

But now the darkness has finally found me, and I'm unable to extinguish the 🔥 that is currently reconstructing my new home. My eternal companion is an ever-present dark shadow guiding me with convoluted commands. The reiterations to have faith in the fall, despite the failure rate and trusting my fear to pilot me.

Through the misinterpretation grows an anticipation for this void of nothingness. I can feel it in the air. It's the moment of dread. The 🔥 storm sparking my spirit has dampened, allowing the darkness to bleed out. I'm ready to accept my fate. The experience isn't new; I usually get on my knees and pray for another miracle, but I'm almost certain my allotment has been reallocated. It's the penalty for wasted blessings I've been too afraid to claim.

Self-diagnosed with self-doubt and sentenced to self-imprisonment, I'm listening to records of degenerative self-reflection. The melodies of misery are suggesting I'm still alive, just dead inside.

The lyrical tune is painful to my soul; failure after failure followed by infinite faults, forcing an examination into fatality.

The recipe to remedy this burden resides in my blurred vision. It requires belief in God-given abilities to live up to a "Premature Promise" to maximize all that I am. The dilemmas are the distractions, distortions making it tough to distinguish between revelation and delusion. Growth is the only prerequisite to defeating whatever's stalking me. Scaling higher heights entails an unapologetic gladiator-style assassination of this shadow character, an ominous transformation to coexist with a self-indulgent variant. Weaponized with generalized anxiety, my soul awakens with an altered ego, eager to fight. Its emergence enlightens the one path aiding the ascent from the impending catastrophe, but the corridor is draped in danger and distress and decorated with dysfunctional views. The excursion to escape the inescapable leaves me scathed with mental impairments, testing my resolve. It leads me to the safety of a panic room, where I'm restricted to clashes with the greatest version of myself! With hundreds of thousands in attendance, my social anxiety reproduces an overload of irrationalities just as another confrontation arises. But this time, the results are more encouraging, and the message fully filtered. Hope heals Despair; Faith fights Fear; Love hinders Hate; Truth infects Deceit; Empathy avenges Vengeance; Open-mindedness presides over Prejudgment; Fulfillment conquers Greed; Envy enjoys Gratitude; and Forgiveness evicts Judgments.

Paralyzed by sleep, I relax my mind and relinquish control, surrendering to the source of it all. Although the warfare persists, there's solace in the solution. Allow my Dreams to be Greater than my Fears. Journey Beyond my Discomforts to Discover my Purpose. Chase my Dreams, Conquer my Destiny, and Create my Legacy. In the end, it's my short story. A short life I'm conceding to the unknown. When I retell my story, I'll tell it with knowledge of its conclusion. God remembers the premature promise, so I'm able to calm ego. But then again, MayBe i'M iLL.

MAYBE I'M ILL

MayBe i'M iLL for trying to rewrite my truth from a mind mangled with mysteries. It's a tedious task, and somewhat dysfunctional, but it's my passion project. I'm too emotionally invested to stop. Comprised of concepts, included within clues buried deep within the context of unconsciousness, I'm attempting to rearrange thought-provoking melodies to help calm my mind. MayBe i'M iLL for believing in my own legacy, chasing a dream while a being pursued by a nightmare. I can't imagine a greater challenge than a mental alliance in the midst of these irrational confrontations. I should neglect this assignment, but there's something great residing inside of me, mixing with my murkiest memories. MayBe i'M iLL with optimism for trying to depict a paradoxical predicament that's being persuaded by the principal of parsimony. I know it's delusional, but it's my passion project. I'm too emotionally invested to stop now. An amateur perfectionist, dismantling my disorder in an articulate fashion. I'm confronting my visions and recruiting them as my first clients. The concise conception is my life's story, neurotically narrated to impersonate a mystical journey to my life's legacy. The deformed pyramid of words are my mountainous ups and downs. Although somewhat unbalanced, the complicated process of simplifying my complexities from a neurotic state of mind is producing stillness from rearranged thought-provoking melodies to help merge my psyche. Initially, the thoughts are repetitively looping before eventually becoming harmonious! My goal as a coauthor is staying present-minded while telling past and future stories in the present tense. I'm nuts, but I'm too emotionally invested to stop now. The more layered the story, the more distorted it feels.

MayBe i'M iLL for believing this product properly illustrates my deformities, but I'm sold on these powerful words generating positive messaging to those who can relate. It's my pregame playlist. MayBe i'M iLL for ripping up the original version, it was just a One-Pager. This time I'll take notes regarding my process of simplifying the complexities of Occam's razor to unravel my distorted thoughts. That's a mouthful, but I view it as a challenge. I must turn around and confront the shadow. I grab my notebook just in case I need to journal my thoughts on techniques and tools required for my success. MayBe i'M iLL because it has taken twelve years to start this project, and less than half a year to finish. You may call it procrastination. Occam's razor is a principle stating that if two competing ideas can explain the same phenomenon, one should use the simpler one. In philosophy, it's a problem-solving principle that recommends searching for explanations constructed with the smallest possible set of elements.

To restate my purpose: I'm looking to construct a comprehensive story on the principle of parsimony, using powerful words in the simplest terms. I have a message that may assist others with their internal struggles, but it's problematic. In order for the words to reverberate with the reader, client, and unbelievers, I must neurotically narrate my thoughts and paint a picture of a psychoneurotic mind in a calm state. This is a story of an overanxious juvenile's journey derived from his journal entries. It's meant to feel convoluted, to mimic twisted thoughts of a traumatized teenager. His entire thirteen years have been 1-B.i.G. Nightmare. This creative editorial format is the only way my story works. It's a purposeful attempt to encourage more individuals to journal. The entire text is encrypted to mimic the mix of fantasy and reality.

MayBe i'M iLL for searching for a better version of myself amongst these mental deformities and negative behaviors. I'm neglecting all logical pathways. Hibernating in inactivity, I'm contemplating a decision to surrender to this irrational course. The afterthoughts of an altered ego, following the intervention of the iD and Superego and their fundamental differences. The story starts twenty years from the beginning with an infinite entendre viewpoint leading to the same feeling. I can't believe I'm here. Telling this tall tale is a tough task; sorry it has taken so long. The formula to my unbalanced mind is illustrated in my story. The riddles are buried too deep to properly resolve. The book is written in pieces. I'm chasing My Shadow, who's currently time-hopping through different dimensions. I'm following, alone, with the darkness attacking me from different directions. It's a manipulative experience! I'm attempting to publish a project with multiple perceptions, each one uniquely catered to the reader, leading to their perfect perspective. It concludes with the personal playlist produced by a thirteen-year-old. It's his Neurotic Narration for Advocation. MayBe i'M iLL for thinking I can make sense of all of this. If the message is to be credible, through the multiple illusions, only one conclusion is concrete. My Father honors his premature promise.

A GOOD MAN'S FATHERLY ENCOUNTER

I heard through a family source: my father is in hospice. I'm told if I want to meet or speak with him, it is to be our first and only encounter. I don't wanna face this man; I despise this man because I missed this man! My heart is breaking as I type these words. After thirty-five years, I never fathomed ever seeing this man. I refused to acknowledge this man once I learned he'd only lived minutes away from me for most of my childhood. From my perspective, he refused to acknowledge me as well, making us even.

I can't remember who told me that my father was near death and that now was the time. I didn't physically drop the phone, but I didn't hear another word of the discussion, not excluding my own spoken words. It's an eerie feeling, but I've been here before, paralyzed in the moment and afraid to respond to the fear. It's a confrontation I am forced to endure day in and day out. But I need to go see this man. I'll regret it for the rest of my life if I don't.

The caller also tells me he has dementia, so I don't expect him to recognize me. I'm relieved of that expectation. I imagine he won't remember this visit at all, which makes my decision to see him a lot easier. I expedite the trip to Greenville, South Carolina, the place that birthed me. It's a small city in comparison to the world I've come to know, but it's forever home! Again, not knowing what to expect, *I'll expect nothing,* providing the comfort I need to safely burst through the facility's entrance, into the reception area. My wife checks us in. I don't know what to say to the receptionist. I only knew the man by his initials. I don't even know what his initials stand for, and I refuse to care.

Now I am rushing to get through this moment. Usually, in these instances, I'd turn around and search for the closest exit. This time, I've freed myself of the memories of it all. He is waiting on the other side of the door. Our eyes meet, and he whispers to the nurse pushing his chair, "That's my son," and he's grinning from ear to ear!

The only advice I received from my father is the greatest gift I've ever gotten. It's the power of forgiveness. As he tells it, he forgave himself a long time ago.

How poetic: my baby boy is peeking through my office door, waiting to make a request. He wants to watch *Five Nights at Freddy's* when I'm done with whatever it is I claim to be doing. I'll continue this story at a later date. I'm going to cherish time with my son!

André Goodman

National Counselor's Exam

Part 5:
A Good Man's Prerequisite

I am terrified of failing this upcoming exam. It isn't just a test; it's the test. It is the key to my tomorrow. The dilemma, however: I've rediscovered my passion for reading and writing. Before falling into this slump, both were favorite recreational activities I used to calm my unprovoked general anxieties. I'm hopeful this test sets the stage for the life I've requested. You'd think I would have this figured out by now, but I am unable to will it. This master's program in clinical mental health counseling is an enlightening experience, but I need a break. While studying for this exam, I'm realizing the text is confirming my neurotic nature.

I hope this isn't another episode, but I can't escape these thoughts paving pathways to an alternative aspect, seemingly related to my diagnosed dysfunction. Truth be told, my nights have been sleepless since deciding to confront this war brewing within my mind. I am a man working to reconcile with myself after suffering multiple mental meltdowns. It's hard to admit, but I'm told denial is the first hurdle. I've broken down the barriers of invulnerability and lowered my standard of perfection since falling short of becoming who I'm called to be.

I did not expect the shock to my nervous system to be as brutal as it's been. I'm not anticipating a full recovery, but I will at the least attempt to forgive myself for any pain I've caused others. So, I sit with your words as you exit the room, and I think back to the promise I made to you a while back. My greatest fear is wasting my life without having served my purpose. Legacy means everything to me. But I'm hindered by my naturally introverted personality. It's my predicament. According to Myers-Briggs Personality Type Indicator (MBTI), I am entrapped in a dichotomous dimension known as the INFJ—an Introverted, Intuitive, Feeling, and Judgment—jail. Supposedly, it is a rare type, making up less than 2 percent of the general population. Based on research and results, INFJ personality types are good advocates and counselors.

It is the mountain I have chosen to climb on a quest to gain access to higher magnitudes of consciousness, hoping to uncover the grace and mercies needed to forgive myself for my shortcomings. This is a precondition to attaining the courage to plead my case of forgiveness from you. Sorry it has taken so long, but I lost desire along the way. My passion for wordplay dissipated when my pen only produced hollow syllables. I thought I had a gift for storytelling, and I thought my name meant something. A Good Man is how it reads, yet I'm unable to believe in its assigned title. It's a f***ed-up feeling, losing a sense of self. I don't sleep much. I dwell in hibernation. It's a long-*ss time to be imprisoned in a void of "RESTlessness."

The confrontation has rendered me completely confused. What follows is a one-on-one interrogation and investigation into self. A neurotic narration of exploration, with illustrations of my mind's dysfunctionality. It's the solution to the situation in which I find myself. A sample of my greatest hits. I'm going to grab a drink. This is a difficult read, a tough listen, a hard share, and an even more strenuous life. I'm embarrassed by all that I am and everything I've become. Yet and still, I love me some me for continuing the fight.

A GOOD MAN'S UNCONVINCED SPOUSE

I'm convinced she isn't convinced as to why it's taken so long to tell my story. I'm dealing with my demons daily. I still have ambitions of chasing my dreams, but they're cloaked with invisibility. If I don't turn back and confront the conflict, I'll be stagnant forever. I don't know who I am right now. I'm experiencing an identity crisis, and these thoughts are increasingly troublesome. As the fight ensues, a journal of illustrations begins fleeing my mind. Sketches of a juvenile's repressed memories.

Amid the conflict, I'm lost within myself, contemplating death as a better option. The internal discussion attacks three parts of my psyche, becoming a mental matrix of mind manipulations. The Mental Matrix, making the maze of mental mystery more multi-faceted. Within it lies my legacy, the story of my process. I have a love affair with music for painting my pain with such beautiful artistry. My playlist is articulated with precision! I'm inspired to fight against the resistance, and although authoring this story is a pipe dream, it's better than living in this self-inflicted misery. Naturally quiet, I'm a deadly danger to myself and others. A Silent, Enigmatic Raconteur.

A GOOD MAN'S MESSAGE

Have faith in the fall despite the failure rate. Trust your fear; let it pilot you. The recipe to remedy your burden resides in your vision. It requires belief in the abilities you're blessed with. You're capable of living up to the premature promise to maximize all that you are. Don't be distracted; distortions are dilemmas only if you allow them to be. Revelations are never diluted; no need to distinguish between misconceptions. Growth is the only prerequisite to defeating whatever's stalking you. It's the energy to keep chasing your dreams. Allow your dreams to be greater than your nightmares. Journey beyond your discomforts to discover your purpose.

Legacy is a life well lived. Failure does not exist if you're doing all you can to succeed. Rest, be still, do nothing. Behind every strong person, there is a story that gives them no choice. A melody of composed mental manipulations is the manner in which my gifts are delivered. Life comes at you hard when you acknowledge your gift, and even harder once your gift begins making room for you. Don't compromise the authenticity of what you share, because it is golden. Forgive yourself for who you're not.

MayBe i'M iLL is a story that has broken me and taught me empathy. It's become my passion project with contents of contentment, reconciling with the darkness. My playlist provides a shortcut through the pyramid of up and downs, turned inside out and remaining nonconformed. The process is monotonous, and self-awareness is key. I'm naturally quiet and unnaturally lethal. A Silent Assassin, one who tells stories with skill.

A LOPSIDED LOVE AFFAIR WITH MY WET DREAM

I'm crushing hard, her soft skin soaking up the sun, the perfect contrast to everything I've already known. The class bell isn't coming fast enough; I need to steal a quick glance. It's her gaze that glamorizes the guilt of my lustful feelings. She's been receptive to my initial maneuvering, carrying her books from class to class while communicating and comparing family dynamics. This infatuation is getting the best of me, doing any and everything I can to be near her, even getting shot at by another one of her admirers. Luckily no bullets struck me, so I return the next day. I'm not allowing the slugs to block my blessing. I'm displaying all my best moves on the basketball court, trying to get her attention, and it works! Next thing I know, she's pulling up on the block, looking for me to express the admirations she's had long before I ever noticed. She tells me she's free from all others, and I believe it because our sensations are blossoming. I hate to see her leave. Watching her walk away creates minor insecurities. Her fan base is enormous, but I give two f***s about the interest of others; I know how to treat a lady because I was raised by three! Some may feel she's dating down, but that's just because they don't know me. I work too f***ing hard to look up to anybody, so the competition doesn't exist. I like to cater to this woman, ensuring she feels special. Why would I ask her to settle for less? If you can take her from me, then that's on me for falling short of what she deserves, and I can respect her wanting better. But because she looks like my future, I'm refusing to take her for granted…promising to explore the world's history. F***, I love the way she owns the room, although I pretend not to notice. Instead, I'll offer her a drink and a cozy seat. Her comfort has become my number-one priority. I thank her for allowing me room to roam freely because it's all I know. I assure I will not abuse it. My preference is being with her always, but respecting each other's boundaries seems healthy to me?

Apologies for the rambling, but I need to specify my adoration. She is my everything!

Apologies for the scrambling, but I was honestly lost. I know it weighed on her patience.

Apologies for pretending not to understand the complaints; they're all completely justified!

Apologies for the length of time it's taking to write this apology, but if I deliver on my promise, promise to let me off the hook? Calculating in my course of action, I'm concluding with care.

I'm sending love to my beautiful wife for helping me get better. I promise my mishaps were not deliberate. I'm trying to tell anyone willing to listen, your husband is nuts! MayBe i'M iLL!

Part 6: Shadow in an Empty Chair

In Jungian terms the Shadow is the part of me that I deny, hide, or repress. This repression is placed outside of my conscious awareness for strategic, survival, or adaptive purposes. These are my darker, forbidden thoughts, feelings, or behaviors that I hide from myself and others. It can also be my joy, my creativity, and my passion. I can only contain it for a certain period of time before it inevitably leaks out from my unconscious psyche, into the cold light of consciousness. It's a conflicting characterization.

The psychic energy it takes to contain my Shadow eventually breaks down. The unconscious will surface and reveal what's hidden, whether it be dark or light. These buried versions of me are explored in isolated psychotherapeutic corners, holding the key to unlocked potential. Yet with the proper support, I can start to reveal, integrate, and embrace these parts of myself. Trusting this natural process of my own feedback toward wholeness is time-consuming, but attacking this process consciously before the dark night of the soul unfolds is a healthy solution in avoiding further self-harm.

> One does not become enlightened by imagining figures of light, but by making the darkness conscious.
>
> —Carl Jung

Used in Gestalt therapy, The Empty Chair technique is a therapeutic approach I use to explore and express my feelings toward another aspect of myself. The idea is to have a conversation with an empty chair as though it is occupied by a different part of my psyche. This facilitates awareness of feelings, thoughts, and behaviors in the present. The goal is to help learn to accept and trust my life experience, enabling me to find healthier ways to deal with life's challenges.

The Empty Chair is used to help promote a dialogue with an aspect of my personality, leading to resolution and acceptance of reality. By externalizing internal conflicts, I gain insight, enabling me to gain a new perspective and explore different worldviews. The Empty Chair symbolizes the "other" in a conversation, various parts of myself that need to be addressed through introspection. This will help me understand my emotions and inspires better reactions.

> Nobody can stand truth if it is told to him. Truth can be tolerated only if you discover it yourself because then, the pride of discovery makes the truth palatable. The person most in control is the person who can give up control.
>
> —Fritz Perls

MAYBE I'M ILL BY DESIGN

I've been up all night searching for inspiration, hoping the new me is part of my tomorrow, although it probably isn't. I didn't get much sleep, and my daughter is asking for a ride to school. She wouldn't disturb me early-morning unless it's important. I'm a little agitated because early-morning traffic is just as bad as early-evening traffic, and my demon is a road-rager. It's the only time I've unconsciously put my kids in harm's way, and my wife has slapped me for it. I know I'm f***ed up, and my kids are terrified because their father is threatening to kill a man over nothing.

Glancing over my old headlines, the last few years have been difficult, smothered in self-doubt. I'm currently disassociated from my closest associates, socially unengaged, and I'm losing interest in life. There's an essence of greatness within, but I'm unable to manifest the meaning because it's distorted by my inability to focus. My legacy is on the line, in the lines of these words unspoken. It's easier to tell myself this story because the self-monologue sells itself. It's a disturbing and rewarding experience. The expression of life lived in self-imposed agony unrelated to reality has me stuck again.

Of course, i'LL take my baby girl to school. She's my everything, so i'LL do anything for her. But this particular morning, I leave her unprotected over a personal vendetta. Some young kid antagonizes me, and I'm not in the mood to let it go. The beast within has finally awoken. In an ignorant response to a symbol symbolizing f*** me, I must f*** this young kid up in a high school parking lot. My princess is horrified; she's never seen her father this way. I've suppressed my demons for forty-five years. No negative social media over any negative activity for the entirety of my life, and here I am, arrogantly ready to throw it all away. Like my fourteen-year-old brother, I finally don't give a f*** about the life that used to mean so much to me.

It takes my daughter two weeks to forgive me; she's p*ssed, rightfully so. Publicly embarrassed over something so petty, I've finally lost it, but it only takes me a few days to stop caring. I love my family, but I don't love my life. Without any real meaning, it has no purpose. I suspensefully peek into the dark hallways-2-heLL, the dramatic downfall of A Good Man. The recollections are trampling my spirit. The personal reflections of dreams and nightmares, blended with hope, faith, and love, overruled by the judgment of societal standards. I'm attempting to find purpose in the simplicity of life's complications, but I'm haunted by my demonic assassin. I'm confused by the mirroring image suggesting my destiny resides within the selling of my soul.

I refuse! Although I despise the darkest parts of myself, I know my heart is good, and I make peace with that. I'm convinced I won't be called home until my work is done, and I still have plenty to do: (1) enjoy the simplicities of an authentic life, (2) allow God to author your life, (3) be still, (4) get some rest, (5) take a seat and share your story.

Thanks for listening,

A Good Man

A GOOD MAN'S NEXT SESSION

A Good Man comes in with perplexed premonitions perpetuated by his unrecognizable reality. His fabricated fantasies are inescapable irrationalities. His passion for poetry arouses an articulation of iLLogical iLLusions. Although improperly recounted, his accounts provide him proper relief. A Good Man possesses a grand awareness of his shortcomings but has yet to address what I believe to be the root cause of his condition. Hopefully he's open to couples counseling and discussing his personal relationships in greater detail in our next session. It sounds as if A Good Man has caused unimaginable pain to his loved ones, and in doing so, he's become the man he despised most, his own father. A Good Man did not have a relationship with his father, and for so long he harbored resentment and disdain for the man that never recognized him as his son. It's come back to haunt him, and his Shadow returns for a rematch. The ending is to be continued, but for now…he lives on!

André Goodman

A GOOD MAN'S HALLS-2-HELL

I. Major Depressive Disorder (MDD)
   a. Persistently low mood, decreased interest in pleasurable activities, feelings of worthlessness, lack of energy, poor concentration, restlessness, sleep disturbances.

II. Generalized Anxiety Disorder (GAD)
   a. Unprovoked nervousness, excessive worry, restlessness, fatigue, trouble concentrating, irritability, increased muscle tension, and trouble sleeping.

III. Post-Traumatic Stress Disorder (PTSD)
   a. Reliving aspects of traumatic events, vivid flashbacks, intrusive thoughts and images, nightmares, intense distress at real or symbolic reminders of the trauma.

IV. Attention Deficit Disorder (ADHD)
   a. Trouble focusing and controlling impulsive behaviors (acting without thought of consequences), difficulty paying attention, hyperactivity.

V. Obsessive-Compulsive Disorder (OCD)
   a. Uncontrollable and recurring obsessions, unwanted thoughts, repetitive compulsions.

André Goodman

Tell Me a Story…

Milton Keynes UK
Ingram Content Group UK Ltd.
UKHW050848040824
446470UK00009B/130